W9-CFI-411

In honor
of
Juanita Spanogle
Spine Search
Co-creator

1985-1986

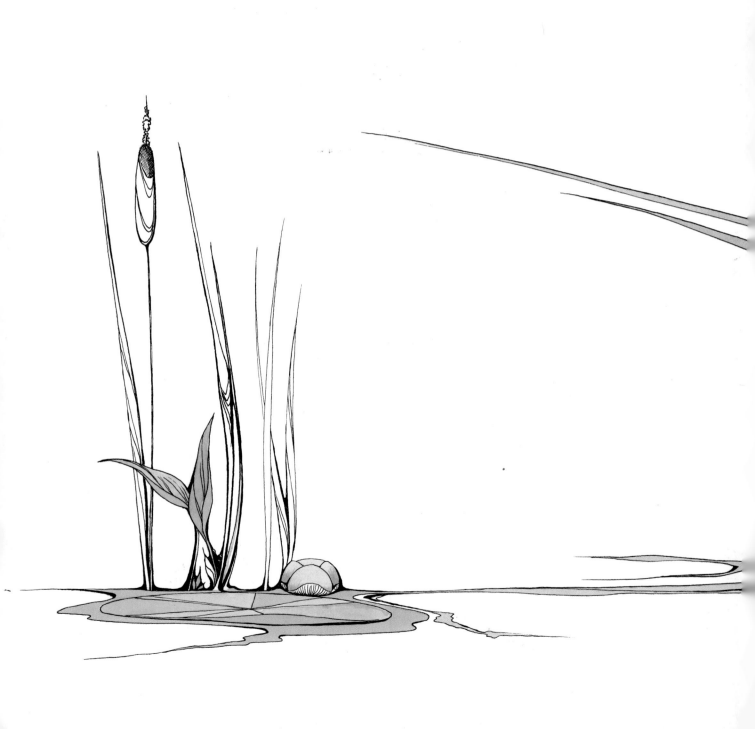

BETWEEN CATTAILS

by Terry Tempest Williams

pictures by Peter Parnall

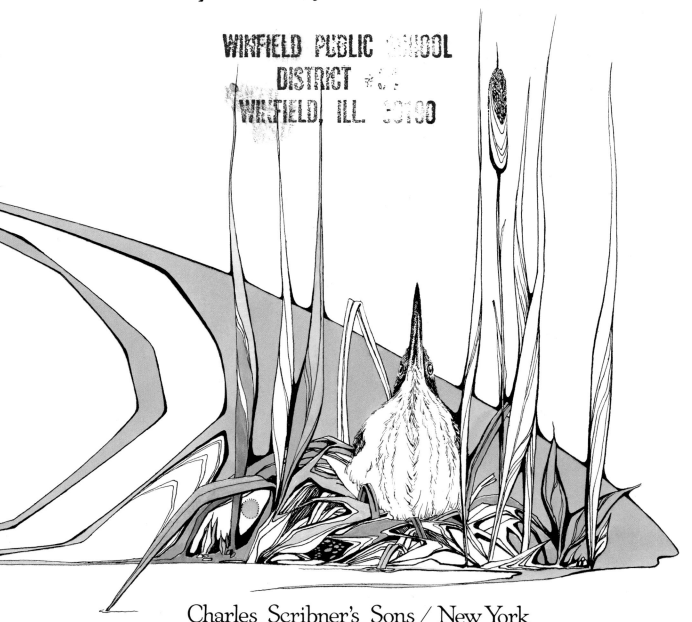

Charles Scribner's Sons / New York

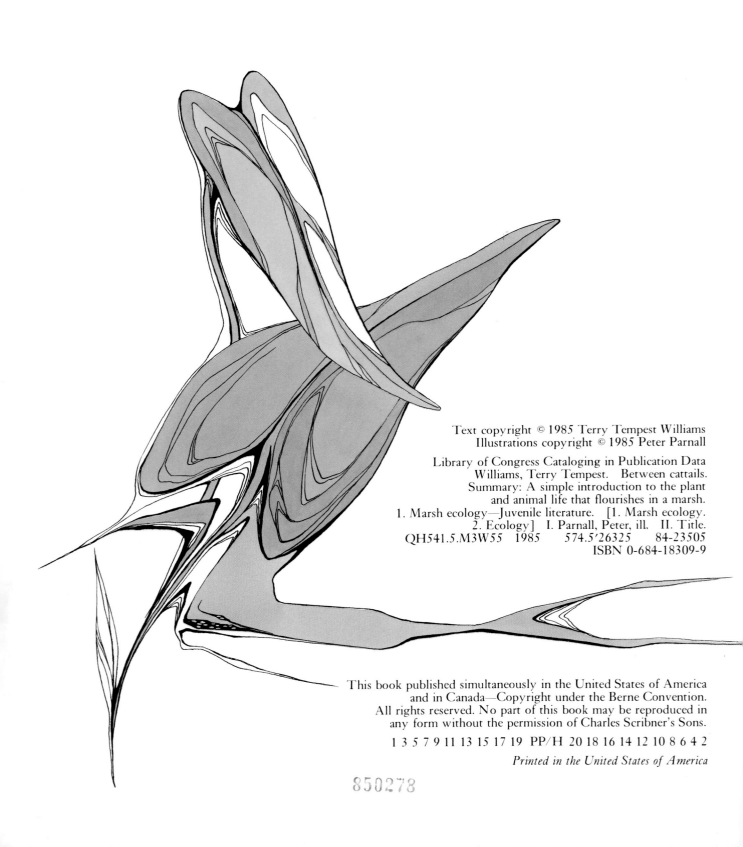

Text copyright © 1985 Terry Tempest Williams
Illustrations copyright © 1985 Peter Parnall

Library of Congress Cataloging in Publication Data
Williams, Terry Tempest.   Between cattails.
Summary: A simple introduction to the plant
and animal life that flourishes in a marsh.
1. Marsh ecology—Juvenile literature.   [1. Marsh ecology.
2. Ecology]   I. Parnall, Peter, ill.   II. Title.
QH541.5.M3W55   1985   574.5′26325   84-23505
ISBN 0-684-18309-9

1 3 5 7 9 11 13 15 17 19 PP/H 20 18 16 14 12 10 8 6 4 2
Printed in the United States of America

For Mimi,
who first introduced me to avocets
and black-necked stilts
at The Bear River Migratory Bird Refuge
in Brigham City, Utah.

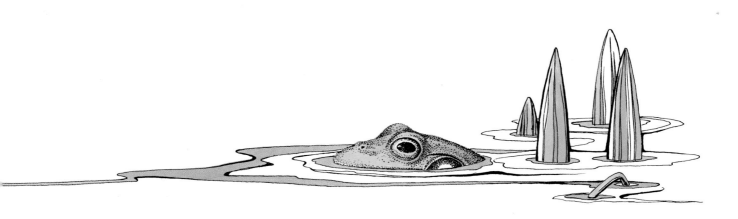

The marsh is an edge
where water and land
meet between cattails.

To enter the marsh
we must separate
the cattails
with our fingers,

step down,
and watch
murky water
seep into our shoes.

We slowly sink
until only our ankles
are visible.

Layers of roots
and matted vegetation
are supporting us.

Red-winged blackbirds
are singing
about home—

As the last cattails are parted,
the marsh opens
and we are looking across
wetlands, bodies of water
that sparkle and sing—

their home of
willow greens,
lily greens,

and water.

"Ko-ka-ree! Ko-ka-ree!"

"Ko-ka-ree! Ko-ka-ree!"

We have found the marsh's pulse. . . .

A long-legged bird
stands motionless
in the clearing.

The water is a mirror.

The eye has not moved—
the eye of Great Blue Heron.

He appears to be studying
what swims below.

Great blue herons
are sentries of the marsh.
They may be found
anywhere there is water,
fishing along edges
with their necks extended
like bent reeds.

Herons fish anytime
but are most active
just before dawn
and at dusk.

They wait
for prey to come
within striking distance
of their sharp, pointed bills—

Lunge!

In the blinking of an eye
Blue Heron spears a sunfish.

We accidentally rustle cattail.
Heron sees us
and flies—

People who live
near the marsh say,
"When a heron
flies from the north,
it is pulling
a storm in
with its legs—"

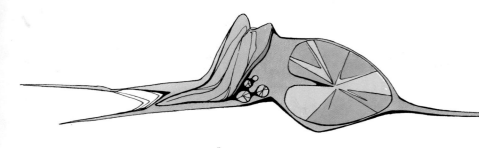

Downwind from Heron,
Muskrat is shredding cattails
for his house.

He is a water rodent,
the marsh specialist
who builds islands.

He cuts and cures,
carries and floats
the vegetation
to his lodge.

In spring, young will be born.
In summer, all will be active.
In fall, food will be stored.

And in winter,
Muskrat will be protected
from heavy snows.

The house of the muskrat
is a habitat
for other creatures, too.

Blue-winged teals
and Forster's terns
nest on top.
Mice or mink or raccoons
may lodge within.

Mites and other insects
live on the plant stalks,
preying and being preyed upon.

Scuds and snails
below the water
devour rotting vegetation
while minnows
find food and shelter
in the passageways.

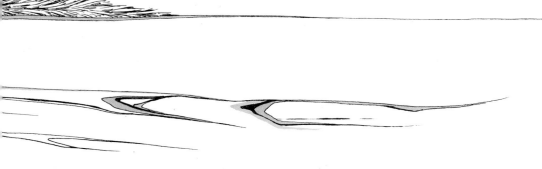

Long-tailed Weasel slips
between cattails.
He has a hankering
for fresh yolks
this morning.

A few yards away,
Green-winged Teal is
probing mud for molluscs.

Her nest is unattended—

Weasel arrives and is gone
before the duck
ever notices
four of her nine
eggs are missing.

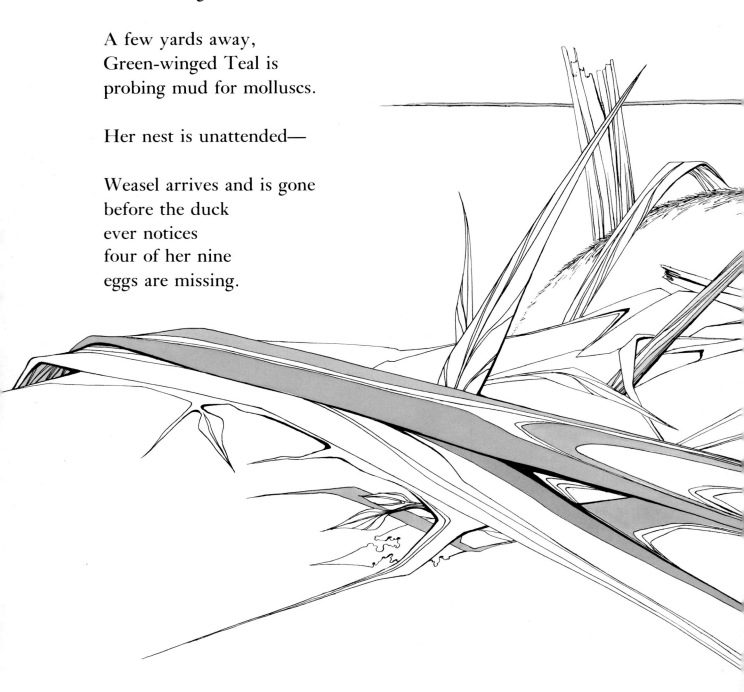

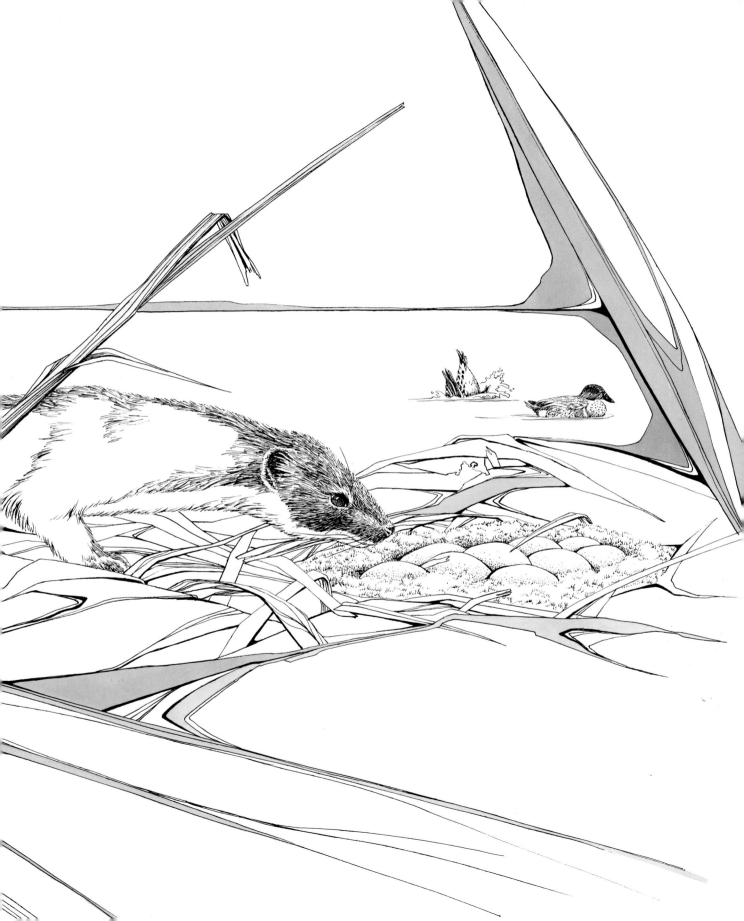

Two Western grebes
ruby-eyed
run side by side
across the water,
feet moving so fast
it becomes a dance.

Their necks arch
and intertwine
in fluid courtship.

This is their "water rush."

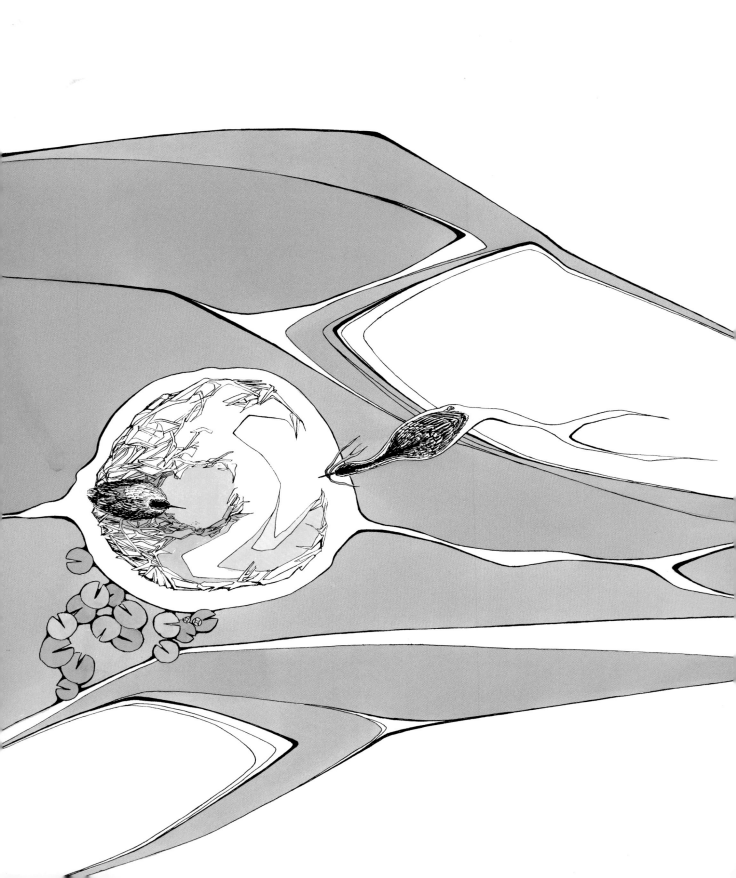

A nest
is in
the making.
A floating island
all their own.

As one bird is consumed,
another is conceived.

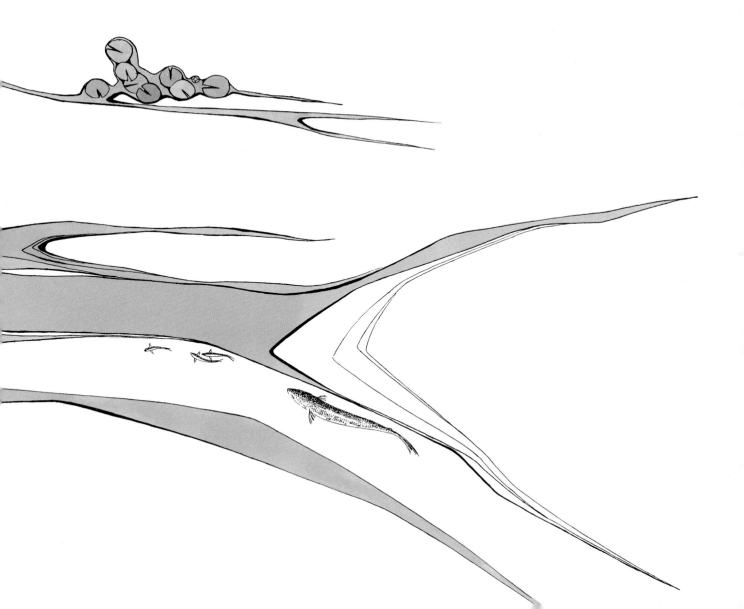

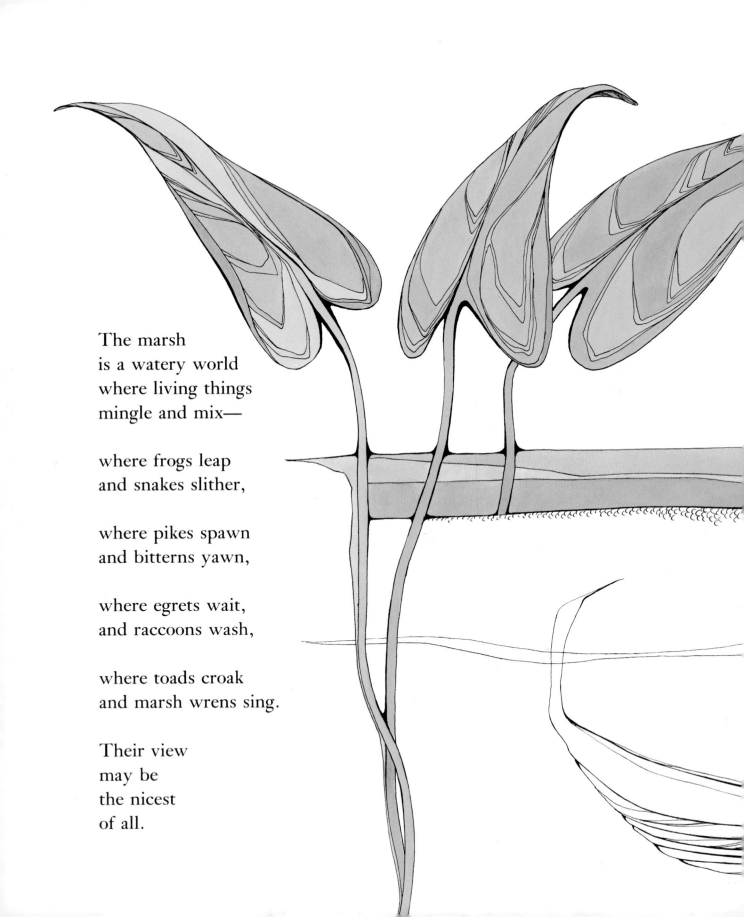

The marsh
is a watery world
where living things
mingle and mix—

where frogs leap
and snakes slither,

where pikes spawn
and bitterns yawn,

where egrets wait,
and raccoons wash,

where toads croak
and marsh wrens sing.

Their view
may be
the nicest
of all.

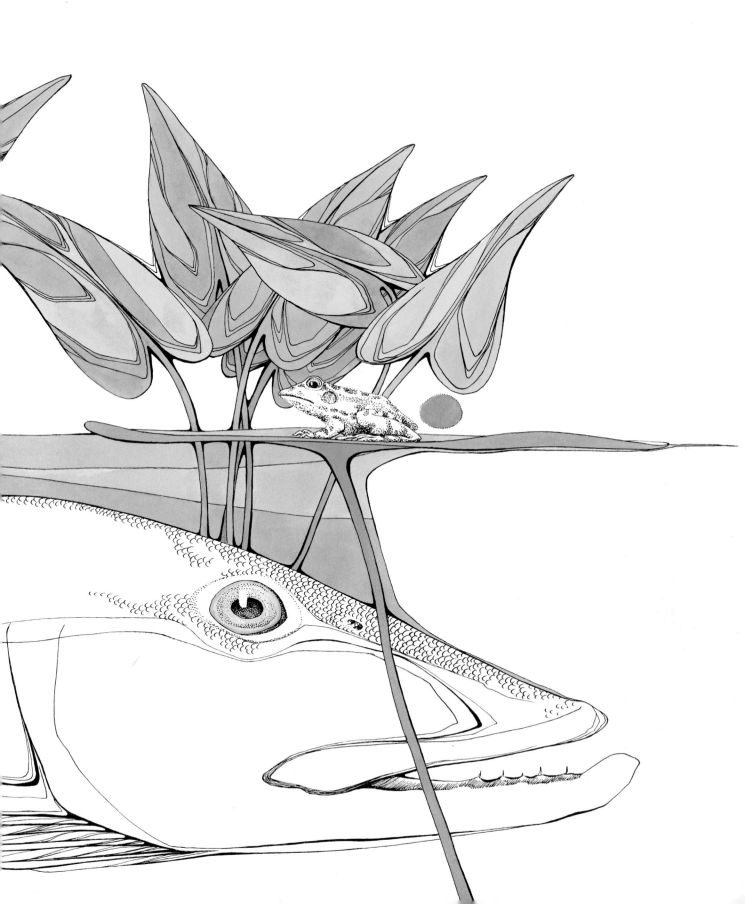

Marsh plants
are marsh producers.

They make food
from the sun,
while becoming food
for others.

Meet
cutgrass
sedge
bulrush
and, of course, cattail.

Their roots grow
in wet soil
or water
all of their lives.

Meet
water-crowfoot
sago pondweed
and widgeon grass.

They are also rooted
in water,
but their stems
and leaves
are covered.

They can capture light
for food-making
in the murkiest of water.

Meet bladderwort
who has an appetite
for tiny crustaceans
and protozoans.
They are snared
in the traps
of green leaves.

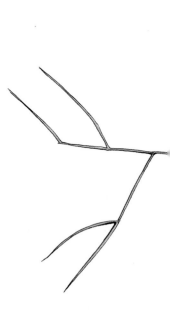

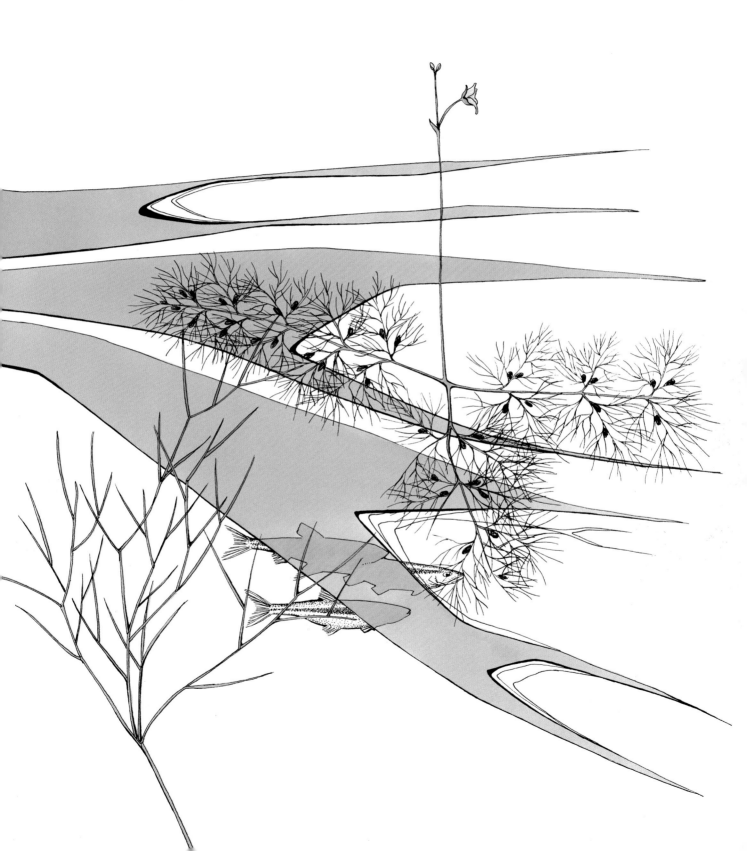

Meet
water lily
with yellow cups
for damselflies
to light on.

Plants like this
are rooted
in deeper water.

They send up
broad, floating leaves
to the surface
where they can hold
sunlight.

Nutrients move
between leaves and
massive roots
through slender stems
that may be six feet long.

Meet
water hyacinth
and
duckweed.

Their roots dangle
in the water
like ribbons.

These are the plants
that create the marsh

that allow the weasel
to eat the eggs

that were laid by the teal
that eats the seeds

that come from the plants
that grow on the edge of the marsh.

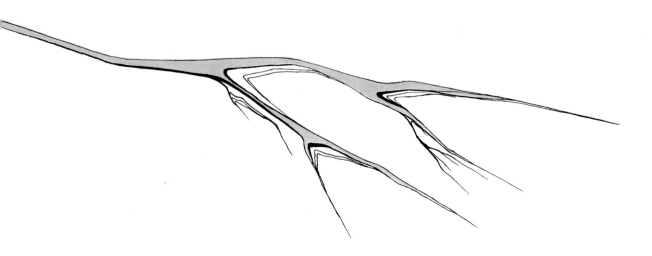

Something else is growing in the marsh.

Inside the water
tiny organisms have just hatched
from hundreds of eggs.
They wriggle and writhe,
    wriggle and writhe.
Their narrow bodies seem to
    touch and release,
    touch and release.

These are "wiggle-tails,"
the larvae of mosquitoes.
They will live in this form
for one to three days,
feeding on smaller creatures
in the water.

They continue to swim.

When full-grown,
in seven to ten days,
"wiggle-tails" turn into "tumblers."

From this pupa stage,
adult mosquitoes emerge.

Barn Swallow
hunts the air for them,
day after day
after day.

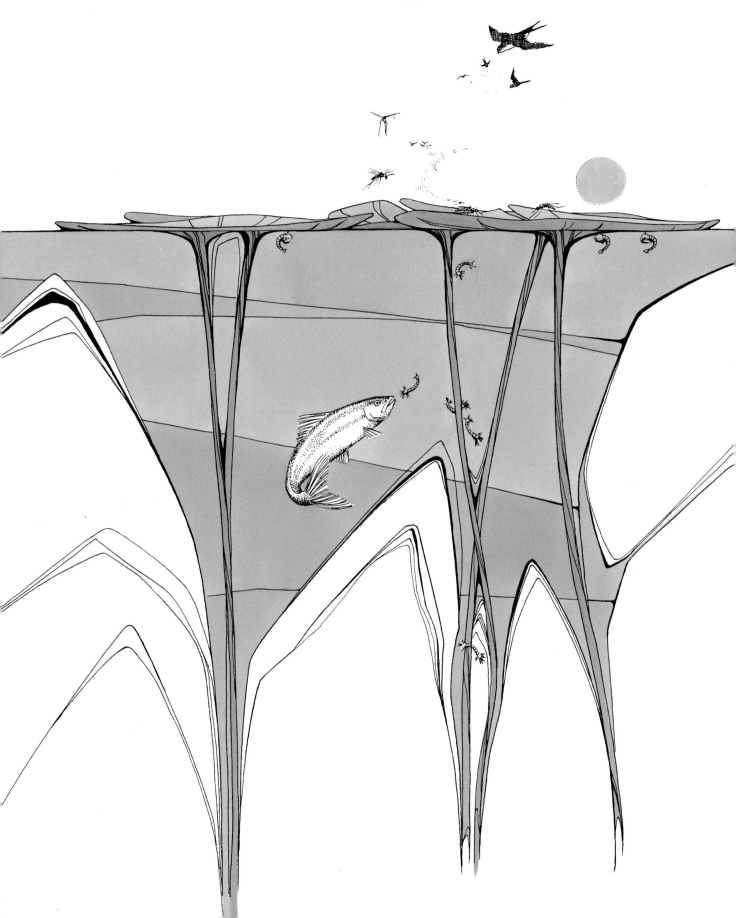

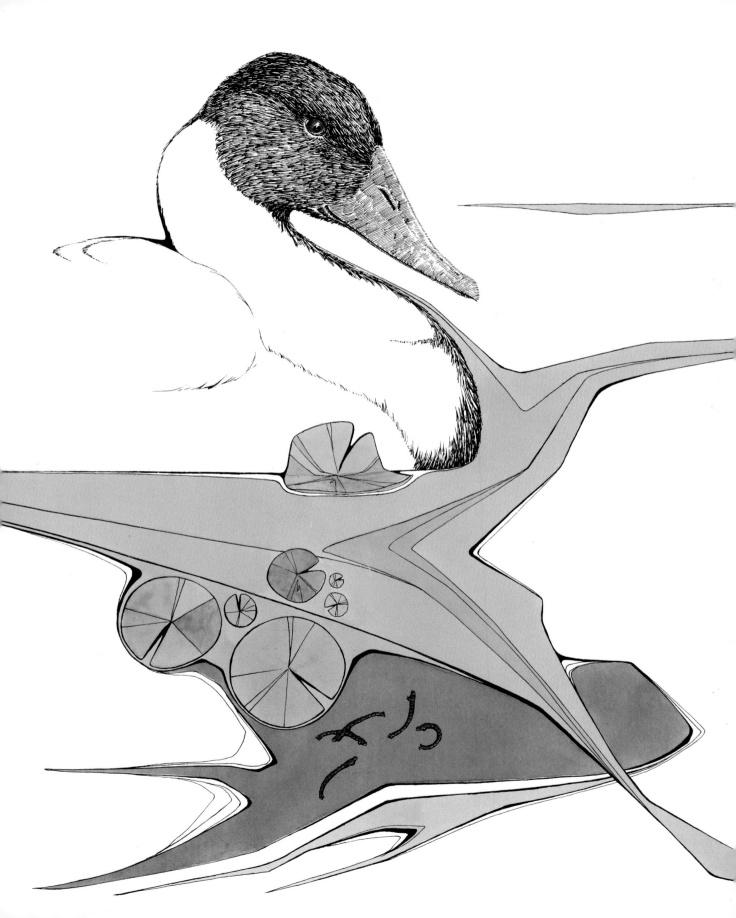

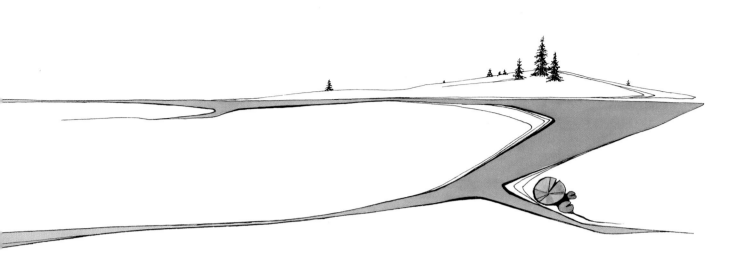

Pieces of red thread
are squirming in the black-bottom
soils of marshes.
These are midge larvae
called "blood worms."

Diving ducks
such as Redhead and Canvasback
eat them.
So do fish and frogs.

Like the mosquito larvae,
midges will pupate
and float to the water's surface.
On another day,
an adult midge will emerge—

Mallard will be there.

Picture giant swarms
rising
like black columns of smoke
against the setting sun.

Midges drone
and hum,
making marsh music.

The marsh
is a fragile habitat,
misunderstood by many—

It is open space
with secret colors,
patterns,
and forms.

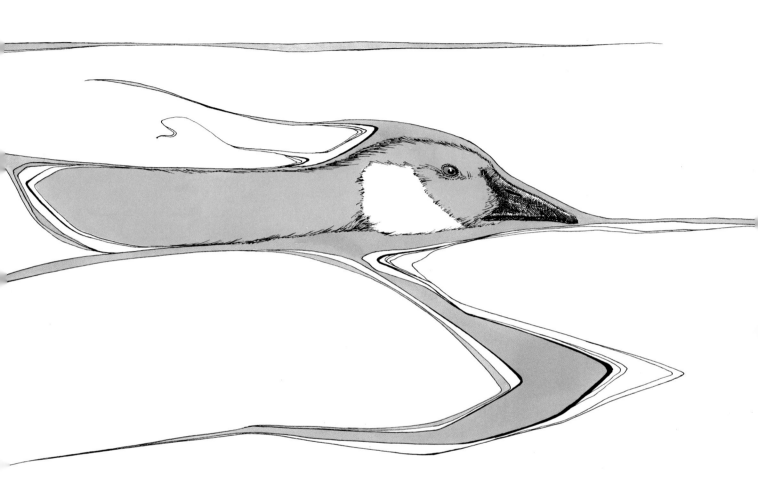

It is where days fly
on the backs
of whistling swans and Canada geese—
Where great waves of wind
move the sky
as wings
crisply fold back
the air.

The marsh is where moonlight dances

on a thousand migrating birds
resting on the water
until it is time
to go. . . .

To save these stories
we must treat the marsh
tenderly.

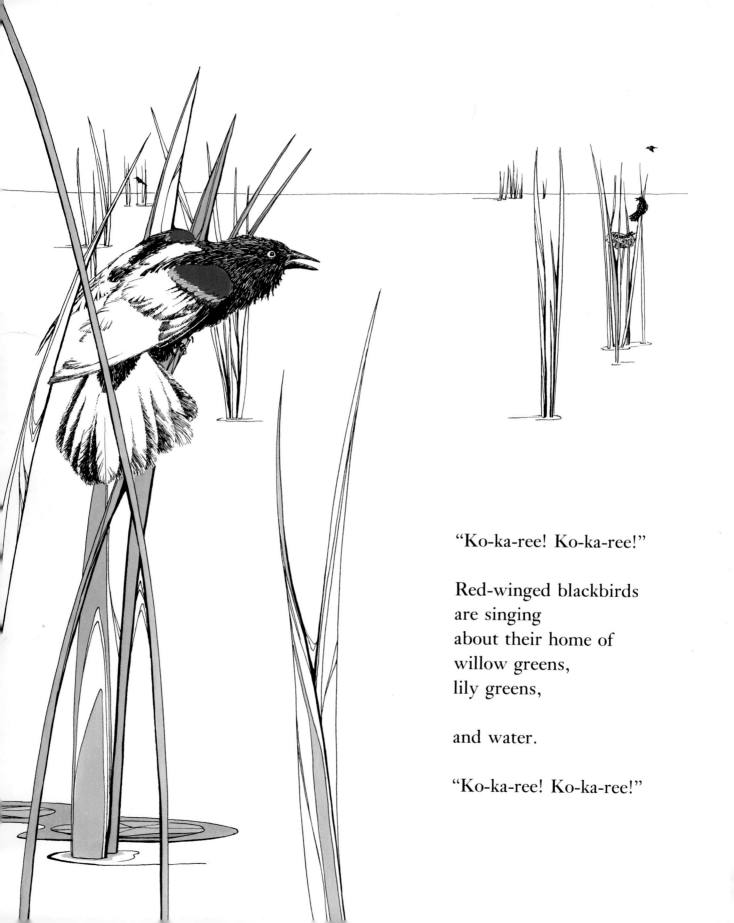

"Ko-ka-ree! Ko-ka-ree!"

Red-winged blackbirds
are singing
about their home of
willow greens,
lily greens,

and water.

"Ko-ka-ree! Ko-ka-ree!"